The Bad Cats of Biddeford

How a band of robber cats took over a small seaside town

Written by Crystal Ward Kent

Illustrated by Denise F. Brown

Any unkind words about dogs reflect the sole opinion of the cats, and do not express the feelings of the author.

©2014 Crystal Ward Kent, all rights reserved

The Bad Cats of Biddeford
ISBN-10:
0985263970
ISBN-13:
978-0-9852639-7-3
Copyright © 2012 by Denise F. Brown, All rights reserved.

No part of this book may be reproduced or transmitted in any form, including photocopying or electronic storage retrieval, without written permission from the author and illustrator.

www.tugboatrescue.com
www.raccoonstudios.com
Raccoon Studios, 692 Sagamore Avenue, Portsmouth, NH 03801 USA 603-436-0788

For my dear kitties, Samantha and Smokey.
Rescuing you was the best thing
I ever did!
You were wonderful friends!

Not long ago, the fair town of Biddeford, Maine was taken over by a band of robber cats. They caused all sorts of problems, as you shall see.

Biddeford is a seaside town of nice shops and quiet streets — not the sort of place where robber cats are common.

These robber cats were strays who had no homes. Some of them had always been strays. They were born on the streets and had never known the love of a family. But a few of the cats had homes once — homes they still dreamed about before they were lost or abandoned. Now, there was no one to feed them; no place for them to keep warm at night or find shelter from the rain. And there was no one to pet them or play the many games cats love.

The stray cats came in all shapes, sizes and colors. They lived under porches and in empty buildings. They slept under cars and bushes. They raided garbage cans and caught rats to eat, and drank water from puddles.

As time went by, the stray cats became tired of their lonely lives and started to live together. It was then that their life of crime began.

One night, after their evening hunt for food, Jocko, a tough little cat with a patch of dark fur over one eye, stood up to speak.

"It is not right that we must live on the street!" he said. "It is time we fought back and made a good life for ourselves."

"But how?" said Mike, a sturdy orange cat.

Jocko stamped his paws. "We will become bandits. We can have nice things even though we do not have people to take care of us. It will be great!"

"Bandits!" exclaimed Mike. "But stealing is against the law. I have never been in trouble with the law. I never even scratched the vet!"

"Do not worry; we will not get caught," said Jocko, licking a paw. "We will be in and out of places before anyone knows what has happened. And if they see us, we will run and climb so fast they will never catch us. Nothing is faster than a good pair of claws!"

The other cats agreed with Jocko, and so, bandits they became.

Jocko

Within weeks, the town of
Biddeford was under attack.

The robber cats broke into
grocery stores and
stole fresh chicken and fish.
They knocked over bottles of milk
and cream and lapped up the puddles.

They raided sewing shops and batted spools of yarn
and threads into hopeless tangles.

They broke into furniture stores to swing on the drapes.

They crept into Mrs. Quimby's plant shop and chewed the spider plants.

In the pet shop, they dabbled their paws in the fish tanks and made the hamster peddle his wheel at top speed.

When they left, the puppies had barked themselves hoarse; the hamster had fainted, and the Bad Cats of Biddeford had stolen all of the cat toys.

One tough old tom cat named Spike carried off a puppy-size chewy bone!

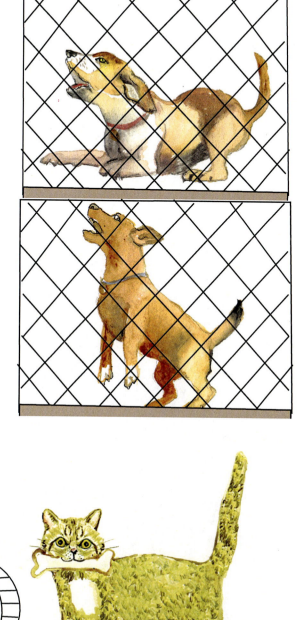

Now their den was a cat's dream!

Little rubber balls, twisty ties and balls of yarn were everywhere.
Crinkly bags covered the floor.
Boxes of cat treats lay tipped over in the corner.
Bits of chewed spider plant were scattered about.
Here and there a baby blanket, carefully dragged from a robbery,
made a bed for a proud bandit cat.

Their life of crime seemed wonderful. The cats had grown plump. They had soft places to nap and toys to play with. They thought they were happy, but deep down, many longed for the one thing still missing from their lives — the love of a family.

Then one day, things started to change. It happened slowly, but the cats' bandit days were coming to an end.

One afternoon, a group of robber cats chasing a squirrel rounded a corner just as old Mr. Jones came around on his bicycle. The sight of a dozen cats bearing down at top speed made Mr. Jones lose his balance and tumble headlong into Mrs. Spinney's garbage cans. There was a great crashing of cans, lids and Mr. Jones' bike, one mighty yell, some screeching meows and scrambling claws, and the scolding of the squirrel, now high in a nearby tree. Then all was silent. After the thundering herd had passed (cats do not run quietly), Mr. Jones rose from the garbage and shouted, "They must be stopped!"

Mr. Jones and the shop owners went to the police. The mayor was called. There was much shouting and fist-waving and the mayor had to bang the table with his gavel to make people be quiet.

"We all know Biddeford has cat trouble," said the mayor. "Bad cat trouble! I have heard about the store damage, the terrified hamster and Mr. Jones' bike accident. I know Mrs. Quimby's spider plants have been chewed within an inch of their lives. I know people are missing tuna fish and yarn and that there is a severe shortage of crinkly bags and twisty ties.

I have heard the good house cats crying because the stores are out cat treats.

Yes, something must be done."

The mayor mopped his round, red face.

"I have talked with Ted, the police chief," continued the mayor, "and he thinks we can solve this cat problem by bringing in some dogs. I am talking about police dogs, smart dogs, dogs specially trained to round up robber cats and things like that.

"Come Tuesday night, these police dogs will be waiting in an alley off Main Street. The minute those pesky cats make a move they will find themselves whisker to whisker with 90 pounds of German Shepherd, and that will be the end of the Bad Cats of Biddeford."

Tuesday night was warm and clear — a purrfect night for prowling, thought the cats, and they took to the streets. They padded quietly through the alleys until they reached Main Street, then paused. Which shop should they rob tonight? But something wasn't right. Two dozen whiskers twitched. Two dozen pairs of ears flicked forward and back, and slowly, two dozen hackles rose.

"Dogs!" hissed Jocko, "It's a trap!"

But before the bandit cats could slip away, the dogs began to bark. They, too, had smelled something on the night air. Cats! They sprang into action. The police and the mayor, watching from cars parked nearby, smiled as the dogs leaped forward.

What happened next was not according to plan.
There was a thudding of paws, a scrambling of claws, and loud howls, hisses and barks. And the bad cats got clean away!

Everyone had forgotten that they were small and swift, quick climbers and master dodgers. They had run over and under, through and around, up and away...leaving the dogs racing in circles and barking at the air.

The cats laughed all the way home, but their chuckles stopped when Snuggles, a plump, spotted cat, came in the next day.
"They have posters with our pictures down at the Post Office," she cried. "They will find us for sure! We must hide!"

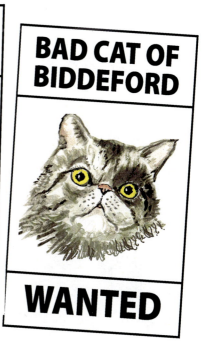

The robber cats hid for many days, but while they hid, a clever trap was
being set. The police had started "Operation Catnip."
Catnip is a wonderful plant that cats cannot resist.
The smell of it makes them first silly then sleepy,
and fills their head with sweet dreams.
The police knew this, and they placed catnip mice on
the floor of the pet shop. Then, they opened the windows and soon
the tempting catnip smell was drifting on the breeze.

The robber cats were dozing in the sun when Snuggles awoke
to a sweet smell tickling her nose. Catnip!
She opened her eyes. Where could it be coming from?
Soon, the other cats noticed the wonderful smell. "Let's go find it!" said Mike,
and off they went.

The bandit cats trotted briskly through their secret backways to the pet shop. Quick as a whisker they were through the open window and rolling about with the catnip mice. None of them thought it strange that the pet shop window would be open with robber cats about.

Soon, all the cats were asleep. A few slept on their backs, a happy smile on their faces. Some lay curled in balls with catnip mice clutched between their paws. Others lay on shelves or draped over boxes.
All were purring and snoring loudly.

Outside, a policeman crept up to the window and peeked in. He smiled at the sight of the sleeping bandit cats. He beckoned to his partners, and before you could say "catnip" they slipped inside the shop and surrounded the cats. The cats were picked up and tucked into carriers. Some snored as they were carried out, while a few woke and meowed weakly.

meow...

Down at the jail, the cats were photographed – full face and profile – and "paw-printed." Then they were put in a cell with the door locked. Two dozen pairs of eyes watched sadly as the jailer walked away, his keys jangling.

Now the mayor did not want to be cruel, and neither did the policemen. When the pictures of the cats appeared in the newspaper – 12 furry faces with big scared eyes peeking out from behind bars — a lot of townspeople began to feel a bit sorry. The cats looked small and lost, not like fierce robbers. What should they do with the Bad Cats of Biddeford?

The mayor hemmed and hawed for several days and tossed and turned in his sleep for several nights. At last, he thought of a solution. He called a lady from a group that protected animals. They took in strays and cared for any creatures that were hurt or sick.

She agreed to meet with the bandit cats.

After several hours in the cell, petting the cats and
talking to them kindly, she came out.
"Why, these are not bad cats," she said. "They are mischievous,
and they were naughty, but they are not bad. They are lonely and lost
and secretly want a good home. No one cared for them, you see.
And when you feel no one cares, sometimes you do foolish things,
and sometimes you do not know how to stop.
"I think these cats just need some love and a chance to do good,
and I know how to give them that chance!" she said.
And off she marched, whistling and swinging her large purse.

When word of the lady's plan got out,
everyone decided the cats deserved some help.

And so it came to be. Some of the cats went to orphanages to play and cuddle with lonely children — children who were once scared and lost like they had been. Others went to nursing homes to bring warmth and comfort to older people, who too often were forgotten as the cats once were. The rest found homes with families where they happily chased balls, basked in the sun, and snuggled close to their new-found families on cold nights.

Even old Mr. Jones had a change of heart. One day he went to the jail to see the cats who had caused him so much misery. The only one left was Spike, the old tom with battered ears and scraggly fur. Yet for all his toughness, he looked small and alone sitting in the cell. Mr. Jones felt his heart soften.

"Why he is a crusty old bachelor like me," he thought. "Maybe he just does not want to be pushed around. I can understand that."

He turned to the jailer. "I will take him! Two old-timers ought to be able to get along!" And off they went, with Spike riding proudly in the bicycle basket.

And that was the last of the Bad Cats of Biddeford.

Today, if you drive through Biddeford, you can sometimes hear a soft rumbling sound. It is the sound of dozens of cats purring happily, for they are finally loved and content.

The End

How You Can Help Homeless Animals

Every year, thousands of homeless cats and dogs are found on the streets. You can help these animals by supporting your local animal shelter.

- Animal shelters are always in need of food, toys, blankets and other items for the animals in their care. Visit the shelter or check out their website to see what items they need.

- Animal shelters are always in need of money to help them take care of the animals. Perhaps your family can make a donation, or you can put on a fundraiser for the animals. Consider a lemonade stand, bake sale, birthday party for the animals or other event that you, your family and friends might do to raise money for the shelter. Your shelter may also have ideas of ways other children have raised funds.

- Consider participating in a shelter fundraiser. Most animal shelters have several fundraisers every year and many of them are a lot of fun for families. Try making it a family tradition at your house. It is a great way to have a good time and help the animals.

- Consider adopting a shelter animal. Shelter animals make wonderful pets and are always forever grateful to those who give them a home and love. Adoption counselors at your local shelter can help you find the dog, cat or other animal that is the perfect fit for your family.

About the Bad Cats of Biddeford

The name of this book came about thanks to a story that ran
on WSCH Channel 6 out of Portland, Maine back in the 1990s.

At that time, Channel 6 had a popular features reporter named Bob Elliot,
who was known for a program called "Bob's Basement."
Elliot covered everything and anything in his shows,
including a story on Biddeford's stray cat population.

At the time, Biddeford had a large number of stray cats
which they were trying to round up, and Elliot did a
tongue-in-cheek story about how they were "wreaking havoc."
He wondered aloud "What would become of the bad cats of Biddeford?"

His broadcast inspired this story.

*The story is a work of fiction and any resemblance to real places,
businesses or people is by accident.*

About the Author & Illustrator

The author, Crystal Ward Kent of Eliot, Maine and the illustrator, Denise F. Brown of Portsmouth, New Hampshire, are frequent collaborators, and this is their second children's book. Kent owns Kent Creative, a creative services agency providing writing, design, marketing and PR out of Dover, New Hampshire. She is an established writer whose work has regularly appeared in magazines such as *Taste of the Seacoast, Northeast Flavor, Coastal Home, University of New Hampshire Magazine, Bay State Builder, Granite State Builder, Yankee* and others. She has also written for the *Chicken Soup* books and *Guideposts* books and is the author of *Mainely Kids: A Guide to Family Fun in Southern Maine*. Animal lovers may recognize her as the author of the popular essay "The Journey" about the special bond between animals and those who love them (www.journeyforanimals.com).

Demise Brown and her husband, John O'Sullivan, own Ad-cetera Graphics and Raccoon Studios of Portsmouth. Brown is the author/illustrator of *Wind: Wild Horse Rescue* adventure book and is well known throughout the region for her stunning watercolors of seacoast scenes, architectural renderings, horse illustrations, and her pony figurine designs with The Trail of Painted Ponies. She is also the creator of the popular series of children's coloring books, *Ted Gets Out*, which celebrates the adventures of one of her cats; a mini children's book, *Abenaki, the Indian Pony*, about a little horse who travels across the country; and *A Deer Visits Nubble Lighthouse*, about a deer who gets stranded on a little island at high tide.

Kent and Brown's first children's book, "Tugboat River Rescue" was released in 2012 and tells the true story of a tugboat rescue on the Piscataqua River. The book has been featured in national tugboat magazines, has a five-star rating on Amazon, and has been the best-selling children's tugboat book on Amazon.

Kent and Brown plan to create additional children's books which highlight their passion for nature and animals.

Made in the USA
Middletown, DE
18 September 2015